S0-AHC-955

How Will Santa Find Me?

Dear Michelle,

My dog likes to sleep in my room but he snores even worse than my dad does! What should I do?

Sincerely,
Can't Sleep a Wink

Dear Michelle,

How can I get my aunt Lucy to stop pinching my cheeks? It hurts!

FroM,
Real Red

Dear Michelle,

My brother wants to hang his lucky sock on Christmas Eve. The problem is, he hasn't washed it in three years! Should I secretly wash it... or trash it?

From,
Stinky's Sister

FULL HOUSE™ Dear MICHELLE

How Will Santa
Find Me?

by Judy Katschke

HarperEntertainment
An Imprint of HarperCollins*Publishers*

A PARACHUTE PRESS BOOK

A PARACHUTE PRESS BOOK

Parachute Publishing, L.L.C.
156 Fifth Avenue
Suite 302
New York, NY 10010

Published by

HarperEntertainment

An Imprint of HarperCollins*Publishers*
10 East 53rd Street, New York, NY 10022-5299

If you purchased this book without a cover, you should be aware that this book is stolen property. It was reported as "unsold and destroyed" to the publisher and neither the author nor the publisher has received any payment for this "stripped book."

TM & © Warner Bros. Entertainment Inc. (s03). All rights reserved.

Full House, characters, names and all related indicia are trademarks of and © Warner Bros. Entertainment Inc. (s03).

All rights reserved. No part of this book may be used or reproduced in any manner whatsoever without written permission of the publisher except in the case of brief quotations embodied in critical articles and reviews. For information address HarperCollins Publishers Inc., 10 East 53rd Street, New York, NY 10022-5299.

ISBN 0-06-054084-2

HarperCollins®, ■®, and HarperEntertainment™ are trademarks of HarperCollins Publishers Inc.

First printing: November 2003

Printed in the United States of America

Visit HarperEntertainment on the World Wide Web at
www.harpercollins.com

10 9 8 7 6 5 4 3 2 1

Chapter One

"Guess what? Now I have *two* things to wish for this Christmas!" I told my best friends Cassie Wilkins and Mandy Metz. It was Friday morning. We were hanging our jackets in the classroom closet.

Mandy slipped hers on a top hook. "What are you wishing for, Michelle?"

"Well, first I want the silver scooter with the pink wheels that I asked Santa for already. And second I want tickets to *The Nutcracker*!" I said, grinning.

Lucas Hamilton and Louie Rizzoli were trading football cards nearby.

Lucas looked at me as if I were from outer space! "Why do you need tickets to crack a bunch of nuts?"

"*The Nutcracker* is a ballet," I told him. "A Christmas ballet. It has dancing toys, dancing mice, and dancing candy!"

I turned to my friends. "My dad drove me to school today, and all the way here he kept talking about what Christmas was like when he was a kid. Every year Dad and his family would make their own presents, eat a huge Christmas dinner, then get all dressed up to see *The Nutcracker* ballet on a real stage!"

"Sweet!" Mandy said. "The only ballet I ever saw was my sister's recital."

"And here's the best part," I said. "I asked Dad if we could go see *The Nutcracker*—and he said 'We'll see.'"

"Uh-oh," Mandy said.

"What's the matter?" I asked her.

2

"Well, in my house 'we'll see' always means *no*," she explained.

"Don't worry, Michelle." Cassie grinned. "In *my* house, 'we'll see' always means *yes*!"

"Well in my house," I said, "'we'll see' means . . . *we'll see*!"

I hope Dad's "we'll see" means yes! I thought. If I got the scooter with the pink wheels *and* went to *The Nutcracker*, that would be the best thing that happened to me all year.

Well, second best. The first best thing was when our teacher, Mrs. Ramirez, gave me the advice column to write in our class newspaper, the *Third-Grade Buzz*. It's called "Dear Michelle." Kids at Frasier Elementary School can write to me with their problems and I write back and try to help them.

Mrs. Ramirez clapped her hands for attention. "Class!" she called out. "Take your seats so we can get started."

We all raced to our desks. I sit in the third seat in the third row. On my right is Sergei Petrovich—the new kid from Russia. On my left is Mandy. Behind me is Spencer Erickson. And in front of me is Julia "Bossy" Rossi. She thinks she knows everything.

"This morning we'll be working on the next edition of the *Third-Grade Buzz*," Mrs. Ramirez told us.

Cool! Working on the *Buzz* meant picking a new letter from my "Dear Michelle" letter box. And the best part—answering it!

"You can work on your stories or drawings for the *Buzz*," Mrs. Ramirez went on. "Bailey, start writing your sports column, Jeff, come up with something funny for your joke column, and—"

"Mrs. Ramirez!" Julia cried. "I already finished my Christmas cookie recipe for the *Buzz*, and it's perfect. What should *I* do?"

"Well, Julia," Mrs. Ramirez replied, "the

hamster cage needs cleaning. Why don't you work on that?"

Julia stomped over to Swifty's messy cage, and I started to giggle. Julia hates cleaning that cage more than anything!

"Michelle," Mrs. Ramirez said, "don't forget to choose a letter for your column."

"I'm on it, Mrs. Ramirez!"

"Okay, class," our teacher went on, "you all have permission to leave your seats while you work on your assignments."

In a flash I was in the hall. My "Dear Michelle" letter box sat on the floor right outside our classroom door. It was decorated with glitter, paper hearts, and the words *Dear Michelle* that I had cut out from purple construction paper.

I carried it to my desk and I gave it a shake. It sounded like it was packed with letters. When I turned it over, tons of them fell out. I was right!

"Wowie-zowie!" I gasped.

Cassie and Mandy came over to watch.

So did whiny Elizabeth Weaner. "You got *millions* of letters, Michelle," she said. "You'll *never* be able to read them all in time."

"Sure, I will," I said. "I'm a fast reader!"

I opened the first envelope. It was a nice Christmas card from Bailey. Then I found a Popsicle stick with a funny message written on it: *Help! I can't stop eating Popsicles! Signed, I.C. Lipz.*

I'll bet Jeff wrote that one! I thought. He's the class clown.

Finally I found a real "Dear Michelle" letter. I smiled as I read it out loud: "'Dear Michelle, I've got a *big* problem. Mom and Dad told me we're going to Grandma's house on Christmas Eve. How will Santa find me? He knows where I live, but does he know where Grandma's house is? And how will he deliver my presents if we are not at home? Can you help? Signed, Been Really Good.'"

"How are you going to answer it?" Cassie asked.

At first I wasn't sure. So I thought of everything I knew about Santa. His workshop is at the North Pole. He has eight reindeer. He knows when you're sleeping and when you're—

"Got it!" I said, snapping my fingers.

I grabbed a notebook from my desk and opened it to a fresh page. "'Dear Been Really Good,'" I said as I began to write. "'Don't worry about going to your Grandma's house. Santa knows when we're sleeping and when we're awake. And he knows if we're naughty or nice. So I bet he'll know where you are on Christmas, too. And that's my advice! Love, Michelle.'"

"There's no way you can give Been Really Good that answer," Elizabeth said.

"Why not?" I asked.

"Because you're *wrong*!" Elizabeth said.

"What are you talking about?" Cassie asked. "Michelle's advice is *awesome*!"

"No way," Elizabeth said. "Once I went to Hawaii for Christmas. Instead of getting the doll I wanted, I got a coconut carved like a monkey!"

"A coconut monkey?" I gulped. "For Christmas?"

Elizabeth nodded. "It was the ugliest monkey I ever saw," she said. "And it was so stinky that my mom wouldn't even let me take it home."

I stared at Elizabeth. There had to be a reason for the smelly coconut. "Are you *sure* there wasn't a coconut on your Christmas list?" I asked her. "Think hard!"

Elizabeth shook her head. "I don't even *like* coconuts! Santa forgot about me, and that's that. Face it, Michelle. Santa didn't find me that Christmas, and he's not going to find Been Really Good either." She walked back to her desk.

"Don't listen to her, Michelle," Mandy whispered. "She's always complaining about something!"

"Yeah," Cassie whispered, too. "Why do you think everybody calls her Elizabeth *Whiner* instead of Elizabeth Weaner?"

"But what happened to the doll that Elizabeth wanted?" I asked. "Did Santa give it to someone else? Do all kids who go away on Christmas get smelly coconuts?"

Cassie and Mandy shrugged.

I thought about kids who go away for Christmas. Did Santa pass right over their empty houses? I slipped the letter into my notebook. "I'm not going to answer this until I'm sure my advice is *right*."

Chapter Two

"Dad, I'm home!" I shouted as I walked into my house after school. Usually I went straight for the milk and cookies, but today the cookies would have to wait. I wanted to tell Dad all about my new letter.

Maybe I'll show it to the rest of my family, too, I thought, and ask them what they think. And that's a lot of people to ask, because I live in a very full house!

There's me, and my dad, Danny Tanner. Then there are my sisters—seventeen-year-old D.J. and twelve-year-old Stephanie. My mom died when I was little, so my uncle, Jesse, moved in to help take care of us. Then he got married to Aunt Becky. And then they had twin boys, Nicky and Alex. Uncle Joey moved in to help out, too. He's not really my uncle, but he's my dad's best friend from college—which is close enough!

Oh, and I can't forget the family's golden retriever, Comet! He's part of the Tanner family, too.

I found my dad in the kitchen. D.J. and Stephanie were there, too.

"Hi, Michelle," Dad said. He was chopping celery at the counter. "Did you have a good day?"

I tossed my backpack on a chair and popped a piece of celery into my mouth. Dad was always trying out recipes for his television show, *Good Morning San Francisco*. Not only was he the host, he was an amazing cook!

"Pretty good," I told him. "I picked out a new letter for my column."

"Can you wait to tell me about it, Michelle?" Dad stopped chopping. "I've got a surprise for you!"

"A surprise?" I said. "Sure!"

"Wait until you see it, Michelle," D.J. said.

Stephanie's blond hair bobbed as she nodded. "It's so cool!"

"Where is it? Where is it?" I asked, jumping up and down.

"We hid it somewhere in the house," Dad said with a grin. "So you'll have to find it."

"We'll tell you if you're hot or cold," Stephanie added.

"All right!" I love guessing games almost as much as I love surprises—and milk and cookies!

I tapped my chin as I looked around the kitchen. Then I started walking slowly toward the refrigerator.

"Is the surprise something good to eat?" I asked.

"Cold!" D.J. called.

"Of course it's cold!" I joked. "It's a refrigerator!"

Dad said I was "warmer" when I left the kitchen. But as soon as I walked into the den . . .

"Temperature's rising!" Stephanie said.

Comet watched me from his dog bed as I searched the den. Could the surprise be under there? But as I passed the coffee table on my way to Comet—

"Hot, hot, hot!" D.J. cried.

I stopped at the coffee table. There was a stack of magazines on top and a wooden bowl filled with nuts.

"You're a thousand degrees in the shade!" Stephanie shouted. "You're simmering! Bubbling! Melting!"

I reached to pick up the magazines. But

then I saw something sticking out from under the bowl. I pulled it out. It was an envelope with the word *tickets* written on the front!

My heart pounded as I stared at the envelope. They *have* to be tickets to *The Nutcracker*, I thought. Why else would Dad have put them under a bowl of nuts?

"This is so awesome!" I cried. "We're going to *The Nutcracker*!"

Dad, D.J., and Stephanie glanced at each other.

"Um, not exactly, Michelle," Dad said. "They're plane tickets. To Grandma's house in Connecticut."

"Grandma's house?" I repeated.

"Grandma invited all of us for an old-fashioned Christmas!" Stephanie said. "She going to cook us a big dinner, and show us her beautiful tree—"

"And she wants us all to make presents

instead of buying them," Dad added. "Just like old times!"

I stared at the ticket envelope. I sure loved my grandma. And I had never gone to Connecticut for Christmas before. Maybe we would go caroling. Maybe it would even snow!

"Yippee!" I skipped around the room. "We're going to Grandma's for Christmas! We're going to Grandma's for Christmas! We're . . ."

I stopped cheering—because I remembered something very, very important.

If we were going to Connecticut for Christmas, that meant we wouldn't be *here*. And that meant Santa might not know where to find me!

Chapter Three

"**I** know what I'll do," I said that night at dinner. "I'll pin a note to Comet's collar. That way Santa will see it when he comes here on Christmas Eve!"

Dad looked up from his salad. "Sorry, Michelle," he said. "Comet will be staying at a friend's house over Christmas."

"Oh," I said, trying to think of something else.

"Come on, Michelle," Stephanie said. "Quit worrying about it."

"What makes you think Santa won't find you?" Aunt Becky asked me.

That's when I told my family all about the letter from Been Really Good and Elizabeth Weaner's coconut monkey.

"Elizabeth said she doesn't even like coconuts!" I finished.

D.J. shrugged. "Maybe one of Santa's elves thought the coconut monkey was a doll."

"Or maybe Elizabeth wasn't very good that year." Stephanie wiggled her eyebrows.

"Believe me, Michelle," Uncle Jesse said. "Santa *will* find you."

"How do you know?" I asked.

Uncle Jesse shrugged. "He's Santa. The big guy knows everything!"

"Oh, yeah?" Uncle Joey tugged on his necktie. It had tiny red and white candy canes all over it. "Then how come he keeps giving me these goofy things?"

Uncle Joey is a stand-up comedian. He is always wearing silly ties and T-shirts and cracking jokes.

"Hey!" Stephanie said. "I gave you that tie!"

Everyone at the table laughed—except me. I couldn't stop thinking about Santa. "But how can he know *everything*?" I asked. "There must be a gazillion kids in the world!"

"You just have to believe, Michelle," Dad said. "Santa will come through—just like he always does."

It sounded like a good enough answer. And Dad was usually right about most stuff. . . .

"Okay, Dad," I said.

"Good," Dad said. "Now let's eat the main course. We're having Connecticut Yankee pot roast in honor of Grandma!" He stacked our salad bowls and carried them into the kitchen. "I'll be right back with the pot roast!"

"All right, gang." Uncle Jesse rubbed

his hands together. "What is everyone making Grandma for Christmas?"

"I think I'll crochet Grandma a scarf," D.J. said. "Those Connecticut winters can get pretty cold."

"Last year at camp we learned how to make bird feeders," Stephanie said. "I'm going to make one for Grandma's backyard."

Nicky and Alex bounced up and down in their booster seats.

"I want to draw Grandma a picture!" Alex said.

"Of Christmas trees!" Nicky shouted.

"Good idea, guys!" Aunt Becky told the twins. She turned to me. "How about you, Michelle? What are you making Grandma?"

Me? I couldn't crochet. I had no idea how to make anything for birds. I liked to draw, but the twins wanted to do that.

"I don't have a clue," I admitted.

I looked at the framed picture of Grandma on the china cabinet. She was so pretty with her long, shiny white hair. . . .

Hey! That gave me an idea.

"I know what I'll do!" I said. "I'll decorate some barrettes and clips for Grandma to wear in her hair!"

"What a great gift," Aunt Becky said. Her big brown eyes shined. "Grandma will love it!"

Cool! Now I didn't have to worry about what to make Grandma. But I was still a little worried about Christmas.

I closed my eyes tight. "Believe," I whispered to myself. "All I have to do is believe!"

"Michelle, would you like to read your letter to the class?" Mrs. Ramirez asked.

"Okay," I said, standing up. It was Monday. I had spent almost all weekend writing my answer.

"'Dear Been Really Good,'" I read out loud. "'Santa knows when you are sleeping and awake. He knows if you've been naughty or nice, too. My family says that Santa knows *everything*. So he'll know where you are this Christmas. All you have to do is keep being good—and believe. And that's my answer! Love, Michelle.'"

"That's what yooooou think," Elizabeth called.

"There will be no more of that, Elizabeth," Mrs. Ramirez said. She turned to me. "Nice job, Michelle. That's very good advice."

"Thanks, Mrs. Ramirez," I said. I was happy my advice was good. But was it *right*?

The recess bell rang and the class lined up by the door.

I stood behind Cassie, who stood behind Mandy.

21

Louie was behind me. He tapped me on the shoulder.

"What's up?" I asked him.

Louie shoved a piece of gum into his mouth. Then he blew a bubble, and it popped over his whole face. "Are you sure about the answer to your letter?" He scraped some gum off his nose. "The one about the kid who is going away for Christmas?"

I glanced at Cassie and Mandy as the line moved out of the classroom. "Yes, I'm sure," I told Louie.

Mandy raised an eyebrow at me. She and Cassie knew that I wasn't totally sure.

"Well, maybe I'm not totally sure," I added.

Louie's whole face drooped. "I knew it," he said as we walked onto the playground. "Now I can forget about that remote-controlled car I wanted for Christmas!"

"How come?" I asked.

Louie jabbed his chest with his thumb. "Because I'm Been Really Good!" he declared.

"How can *you* be Been Really Good?" Mandy asked. "You stuck gum under my chair just last week!"

"Okay, okay!" Louie said. "But since then I've been really good. I promise. You can ask my sister!" He headed toward the monkey bars.

"Wait, Louie!" I said, running after him. "I'm going to visit my grandma in Connecticut. So Santa may not find me on Christmas either."

"What are we going to do, Michelle?" Louie frowned. "It's not like we can just *tell* Santa where we are."

Tell Santa? Louie didn't know it, but he had just given me an awesome idea!

"Why *can't* we tell Santa?" I asked. "We

can write him a letter. Just like we did when we told him what we wanted for Christmas."

Louie stretched the gum in and out of his mouth as he thought. "But Christmas is right around the corner," he said. "Santa may not get our letter in time."

A soccer ball rolled over to me, and I kicked it. "Then we'll put on our thinking caps and think of something quicker!" I said.

"Can Mandy and I help?" Cassie asked.

"Sure," I said. "Santa has helpers, so why shouldn't we?"

Mandy and Cassie cheered.

Even Louie began to smile.

And I had a really good feeling about this. With the four of us working on it, we were bound to find a way to reach Santa!

Chapter Four

"Okay, let's get started!" I said after school. "Who has an idea about how to reach Santa?"

I looked at Cassie, Mandy, and Louie sitting on the floor in my den. I couldn't *see* their thinking caps, but I knew they were wearing them!

"I've got it!" Cassie said. "Why don't we call Santa on the phone?"

"Good idea," I said. "What's Santa's number?"

Mandy shrugged. "Probably 1-800-Santa."

I jumped up, ran to the phone, and

quickly dialed the number. But when I was done, I didn't hear anything. Not even a ring!

"Maybe Santa has another number," Mandy suggested. "Let's look it up in the phone book." She took the big San Francisco phone book off the end table.

"Look under Claus," I said. "For Santa Claus."

Mandy flipped the book open to the C's. "There are a bunch of Clauses," she said. "Mona . . . Nadine . . . Nicholas . . ."

"Nicholas Claus!" I shouted. "As in Saint Nick!"

Cassie jabbed the page. "And his middle initial is S. That's probably for Santa!"

"That's our man!" Louie said. "And he lives right here in San Francisco, California."

"San Francisco?" Mandy said. "I thought Santa lives at the North Pole."

"Let's just call the number and see if

Santa answers." I dialed the number. "It's ringing, it's ringing! What do I call him? Santa? Mr. Claus—"

"Hello?" a man's voice cut in.

"Um, Mr. Claus," I said. "My name is Michelle Tanner and I want you to know that I will be away this Christmas and so will my friend Louie Rizzoli."

"Why are you telling me this?" Mr. Claus said.

"Well, you are Santa Claus, aren't you?" I asked.

At first Mr. Claus didn't answer. Then he began to laugh.

"He's laughing," I whispered to my friends. "But it's ha, ha, ha—not ho, ho, ho!"

"Young lady . . ." Mr. Claus chuckled some more. "My name is Nicholas Claus, but I am not *Santa* Claus."

"What about the *S* in the middle of your name?" I asked. "Doesn't it stand for—"

"Stanley," he said. "My middle name is Stanley."

"Stanley?" I squeaked.

Mandy shook her head. "Not the right guy," she whispered.

"Sorry, Mr. Claus." I sighed. "Have a merry Christmas—even if you aren't Santa." I hung up.

The four of us plopped back down on the floor.

Cassie rested her chin in her hands. "Now what do we do?"

"We forget about my remote-controlled car!" Louie wailed. "And Michelle's silver scooter!"

"We can't give up, Louie," I said. "We're going to find Santa. Even if we have to hook up Comet to my sled and fly to the North Pole ourselves!"

"Okay, okay." Louie sighed.

"I've got it! Why don't we try calling the

North Pole?" I said. "That's a lot easier than flying there."

We didn't have a North Pole phone book, so I did the next best thing. I dialed the operator.

Dad walked into the den just as I pressed the Zero button on the keypad. He gave us a little wave and I waved back.

Then the operator came on the line. "Can I help you?" she asked.

"Yes, Operator," I said. "I would like to call the North Pole, please."

"North Pole?" Dad gasped. He started waving his arms. "Michelle, hang up! Hang up!"

I hung up the phone. "What's the matter, Dad?"

"Do you know how much it costs to call the North Pole?" he asked.

Louie pulled some coins from his pocket. "Will thirty-three cents be enough?"

29

Dad shook his head. "Calling the North Pole is very, very expensive. In fact, whenever you want to make a long-distance call, you must always ask me. Deal?"

"Okay, Dad," I agreed. "But how else are we going to reach Santa Claus?"

"Try the old-fashioned way," Dad said. "Write to him."

After Dad left the den, I turned to my friends. "Maybe we *should* write to Santa.

"It's worth a try," Mandy said. "I mean, a letter *might* get to the North Pole in time."

I remembered the time I wrote to my favorite actress. I sent her my letter and an envelope with my address on it to make sure she wrote back. And she did!

"We'll send two envelopes with our letter," I said. "One with my address and the other one with Louie's. And we'll ask Santa to let us know if he got our message!"

In a flash I wrote the letter. It was ready to be delivered to the North Pole!

The four of us went outside to the mailbox. But just as I was about to drop it inside, I saw something better. "Look! The Speedy Express truck!" I pointed to the blue truck parked on the corner. "If we send our letter express mail, Santa will get it for sure!"

We ran to the driver. He was standing next to his truck with a handful of envelopes.

"Can you take this letter, too, please?" I asked him. "It's going to Santa at the North Pole!"

The man's eyes lit up. "North Pole, huh?" he asked. "Let me make sure I have snow tires so I don't get stuck up there." He circled the truck, checking it out. "Yup! Looks like I'm going to make it! And don't worry about the extra charge for express service. It's my Christmas present to you!"

"Thanks, Mister!" I said, handing him our letter.

We jumped up and down as the truck pulled away.

"Remote-controlled car, here I come!" Louie cheered.

"Silver scooter," I shouted, "I can feel you under my feet already!"

Now all we had to do was wait for Santa's answer. And if we were lucky—it wouldn't take long!

Chapter Five

"Anything from Santa today?" I asked the Speedy Express driver. It was three days since we gave him our letter to Santa. Three *long* days!

"Sorry, Michelle." He sighed. "Nothing yet."

Phooey, I thought. But I smiled at the driver and said, "Thank you. See you tomorrow."

I went back into the house. My sisters were in the den. They were working on their presents for Grandma. D.J. was finishing Grandma's scarf. Stephanie was putting the finishing touches on her bird feeder.

"No luck, huh?" D.J. asked.

"No letter yet," I said. "But I *did* finish five hair clips for Grandma today." I held one up—a barrette covered with tiny seashells and glitter.

"Pretty cool, Michelle!" Stephanie said. She tilted her head and studied it. "But isn't that *my* barrette?"

"Oops!" I thought it was mine. But I guess that's what happens when you share a room with your sister!

I started working on hair clip number six. This one was going to have a plastic rose glued to it. Grandma loves roses!

As I squirted glue on a red clip, I started to think about Santa again.

Maybe he didn't get the letter. Or maybe one of his elves forgot to hand it to him. Or maybe one of his reindeer chewed it up.

Stephanie put down her bird feeder

and walked to the computer. "Time for an E-mail check!" she said.

"When isn't it?" D.J. asked. She pushed her long brown hair behind her ears.

"Hey, D.J., Michelle!" Stephanie called from the desk. "It's an E-mail from Grandma. And she sent us a picture!"

D.J. and I ran to the computer.

I watched Stephanie click on a little picture of a camera. Soon Grandma's picture appeared on the screen.

But Grandma looked totally different. Her twinkling blue eyes and cheery smile were still there. But her long, shiny white hair was *not*!

I gasped. Grandma had cut it all off!

"She wrote us a message," Stephanie said. "It says, 'How do you like my new short hairdo? Love, Grandma.'"

My knees began to wobble. "Sh-sh-short?" I stammered.

"Uh-oh," D.J. said under her breath.

But Stephanie was all smiles. "I think Grandma's hair is cool," she said. "Don't you like it, Michelle?"

"Like it? Like it?" I cried. "Grandma can't use my hair clips anymore. Now I have to make her a new present!"

"You mean your grandma cut her hair short?" Cassie gasped. "After you made all those hair clips?"

"I can't believe it!" Mandy cried.

"Neither can I," I said. "But it's true."

It was Friday morning. My class was in the computer lab working on our newspaper. There were six computers and a printer against a wall. A big table stood in the middle of the room. It was for drawing, pasting, stapling, or for anything else we had to do for the paper.

"Now I have only six days left to make

Grandma a brand-new present," I said.

And Christmas Eve is only six days away, I thought. We still hadn't heard from Santa. I looked around the lab. "Where's Louie? I want to ask him if he heard from Santa yesterday."

I spotted him carrying a stack of papers to the table in the middle of the room. I rushed over to him.

"So did you hear from Santa yesterday?" I asked him.

"Nope," Louie said. "How about you?"

"No," I said.

"What are we going to do, Michelle?" Louie asked. "Christmas is almost here. We have to think of *something*."

"Louie?" Mrs. Ramirez asked as she walked by. "Is that gum you're chewing?"

"No." Louie quickly yanked out his gum and stuck it behind his ear. Then he got up to refill the stapler.

I waited for a computer to free up. I had to type my "Dear Michelle" column and get it ready for the *Third-Grade Buzz*.

Each kid at a computer was working quietly—except for Julia. She was shouting out her Christmas cookie recipe.

"'Santa's Favorite Cookies,'" Julia said. "'By Julia Hannah Rossi . . .'"

I rolled my eyes. Maybe I'll send Grandma an E-mail after I type up my column, I thought. After all, I *do* like her new hairstyle. I should tell her.

But as I thought about what I would E-mail Grandma, I thought of something else! I definitely knew how to find Santa. And soon Santa would definitely know how to find us!

Chapter Six

I ran to the table where Louie was stapling his papers. "I just got an amazing idea!" I said. "Let's send Santa an E-mail!"

Louie wrinkled his nose. "How are we going to find Santa's E-mail address?"

"We won't have to," I said. "Most famous people have their own Web sites. So Santa probably does, too!"

We hurried to Mrs. Ramirez. She was showing Gracie Chin how to scan a picture of her cocker spaniel. The dog was wearing fake reindeer antlers over his ears.

"Mrs. Ramirez," I asked, "can I use the

computer to go online? Please, please?"

"Does it have anything to do with your column, Michelle?" Mrs. Ramirez asked.

Hmm. My letter *was* about Santa. "Yes, it does!"

Mrs. Ramirez nodded, and Louie and I ran to the computers. Lucky for us, Cassie and Mandy were working at one.

"Cassie, Mandy, stop what you're doing!" I said. "We're sending Santa an E-mail!"

"E-mail!" Mandy exclaimed. "Why didn't I think of that?"

"Because Michelle did!" Cassie giggled.

I could see Julia lean in to listen. Too bad her computer was right next to ours.

Mandy stood up. "It's all yours, Michelle!"

I sat in front of the screen and used the mouse to click the word *Search*.

"Type in *Santa*," Louie said. "That should do it."

"S-a-n-t-a!" I spelled as I typed. Next I

clicked *Go* and waited until a list of Santa sites popped up.

"Santa costumes . . . Santa jokes," I read aloud. "Santa ice cream cakes . . . Santa's workshop!"

I clicked on Santa's workshop and waited. We watched as a cartoon picture of the North Pole flashed on.

There were tiny elves carrying toys out of a cottage covered with snow. Santa's sleigh was parked nearby and tied to his reindeer.

"But how do we reach Santa?" I asked.

Cassie pointed to a picture of a snow-covered mailbox. "Try that!" she said.

I gave the mailbox a click. A message box appeared on the screen. It had the words *Send to Santa*.

"Santa's E-mail!" I exclaimed.

I typed my message to Santa: "I'll be at my grandma's in Greenwich, Connecticut. Her name is Flora Tanner," I mumbled.

"Louie will be in Denver, Colorado. His grandpa's name is—"

"Samuel," Louie said. "But Santa can call him Sam!"

"Wait a minute!" Julia cut in. "I thought you said that Santa knows where all kids are on Christmas. So why do you have to tell him where you'll be?"

"None of your business!" Mandy said.

I clicked *Send*, and a box flashed on the screen. It said *Inbox full. Try again!*

"What does that mean?" Mandy asked.

Julia leaned over and looked at it. "Duh!" she cried. "A million kids are probably trying to reach Santa. It means his box is full. No more letters allowed. So why don't you just give up?"

Give up? I wasn't going to let Julia "Bossy" Rossi tell me what to do!

"I'm never going to give up," I said. "Never! I'll find Santa!"

Chapter Seven

"We tried everything we could think of," I told Aunt Becky after school. "But we still haven't found Santa. I don't know what to do next."

Aunt Becky looked up from the kitchen table. She was busy working on her Christmas present for Grandma. "Don't forget what your dad told you." She cut a long pink ribbon. "You have to *believe*!"

I sat at the table next to her. "I guess I'll believe it when I see it," I said.

"See what?" Aunt Becky asked.

"My silver scooter with the pink

wheels!" I answered. Then I smelled something nice. Like flowers.

"What's that pretty smell?" I asked.

Aunt Becky picked up a small bowl filled with tiny rosebuds. They were mixed up with some purple stuff.

"They're dried roses and lavender," Aunt Becky said. "I'm pouring them into little cloth bags and making sachets."

"Sa-shays?" I said slowly.

"It's a French word." Aunt Becky tied a bag closed with a pink ribbon. "Grandma can put them in her drawers to make everything inside smell nice."

She handed me the bag and I held it under my nose. "Mmm," I said. "Grandma is going to like these."

"What are *you* making, Michelle?" Aunt Becky asked.

"Nothing so far," I said. "I can't think of anything."

Aunt Becky slid a magazine across the table. "I got my idea from this crafts magazine. Maybe you can, too."

"Thanks, Aunt Becky." I flipped through the magazine. One page showed you how to make a Christmas wreath out of dog biscuits. Another showed how to make flowerpots out of coffee cans. But then I saw something that made my eyes pop wide open.

"I can do this!" I showed the page to Aunt Becky. "All I need to do is find an old sweater and decorate it to make it look new and Christmas-y!"

"Sounds good to me," Aunt Becky said. "And I'm sure you can find a nice sweater in the big cardboard box."

The big cardboard box was where we put all of the clothes we wanted to give away. Dad kept it in the garage.

"Be right back!" I told Aunt Becky.

Comet followed me into the garage. He sniffed at the box as I dug through it. I found a bright orange jersey with blue trim. It was big enough to fit Grandma. But when I turned it around—

"'Go San Francisco Giants'?" I read. "I can't decorate a Giants shirt for Christmas!"

Comet wagged his tail as I tossed the jersey aside.

"Besides," I added, "Grandma is a Yankees fan."

I dug some more. There were tons of Alex's and Nicky's baby clothes. And some funny T-shirts Uncle Joey used to wear. But way at the bottom I found a bulky blue sweater that used to belong to D.J. It looked practically new.

"It's the perfect sweater for Grandma, Comet," I said, waving the sweater. "My troubles are over!"

But then I remembered Santa. "Well." I sighed. "Almost over."

"'Frosty the snowman,'" I sang to myself. "Da, da, da, da, dum, dum, dum."

It was Sunday. Comet watched me as I sat in my room, gluing a shiny red ribbon onto Grandma's sweater. I had worked on it all weekend and everybody helped me!

Dad gave me an old Christmas tablecloth to cut up. It had cute little snowmen all over it. Aunt Becky gave me her box of buttons and let me use all the green and red ones. Even Stephanie pitched in. She let me cut up her old white ice-skating skirt. I snipped around the cocoa stain and made a bunch of lacy snowflakes!

"Grandma's sweater is going to be perfect, Comet," I said. "Now, if I could just think of the perfect way to reach Santa." I petted Comet's head.

Maybe we could write our message on a huge balloon—the kind they use in those holiday parades, I thought. Except where would we find a balloon like *that*? Or we could flash our message on that gigantic screen in the baseball stadium. . . . But it's not baseball season, I remembered.

I'm *not* giving up on reaching Santa, I thought as I snipped, sewed, and glued almost all day long.

"Awesome!" I held up the sweater when I finished it. "Grandma is going to love it!"

"Hey. Isn't that my old sweater?" D.J. asked.

I turned and saw her standing at the door with her backpack over one shoulder.

"It *is* your old sweater, D.J. But I decorated it with all this neat Christmas stuff. And I'm going to give it to Grandma for Christmas," I said.

48

"Um, it looks really nice," D.J. said.

"The sweater was almost like new," I said. "Why did you want to give it away?"

"It kind of . . . itched," D.J. said in a small voice.

"Itched?" I gasped. "Did you say . . . itched?"

It didn't feel itchy to me. But itchy sweaters never felt itchy—until you put them on and had to wear them all day. Then it was too late!

"It wasn't that bad, Michelle," D.J. said. "I just got a little . . . rash."

"A rash?" I cried. "I can't give Grandma a rash for Christmas!"

I flopped back on my bed and stared at the ceiling. Christmas was four days away and nothing was going right. . . .

And I thought this was the season to be *jolly*!

Chapter Eight

"Here it is, class," Mrs. Ramirez told us. "The new edition of the *Third-Grade Buzz*!"

Everyone cheered as Mrs. Ramirez handed out copies of our newspaper. It was printed on bright green paper this time—just for Christmas.

"Here's your column, Michelle," Louie said. He held up his paper. "And my letter, too."

I turned to my "Dear Michelle" column and forced a smile. I wasn't too excited about seeing it this time. Probably because I still wasn't sure of my answer.

But everyone else was buzzing about their stories. Bailey's sports column was about the jump-rope contest in the school yard. And how the champ had gotten her ponytail tangled in the jump rope. Ouch!

But the class loved Lucas's story best. It was called "The Elf Diaries—Behind the Scenes at Santa's Workshop."

Lucas was so proud, he read it out loud: "'Dear Diary. Today we caught Binky sleeping on the job. So if a bunch of kids get skateboards with square wheels, or dolls with teddy-bear heads—it won't be *my* fault!'"

Page Alexander raised her hand. "Mrs. Ramirez? Is Lucas's story real? Or did he make it up?" she asked.

"He made this one up, Paige," Mrs. Ramirez said. "And stories that are made up are called fiction. It's nice to have fiction in our newspaper once in a while."

Julia walked over to me. "I just thought of something, Michelle. You were trying to reach Santa to tell him you'd be away."

"So?" I asked.

Julia held up her copy of the newspaper. It was opened to my "Dear Michelle" column. "So you didn't believe your answer about Santa!" she said. "That means your column must be . . . fiction!"

"Is not!" I said.

"Is *so*!" Julia replied.

"Julia?" Mrs. Ramirez called. "Why don't you go to your seat and read the paper silently?"

Julia walked back to her desk, but she glared at me all the way.

"Don't listen to her, Michelle," Cassie whispered.

"Julia is just jealous," Mandy said. "She wanted her own advice column."

"I know," I said.

Louie sighed. "I just wish there were still a way we could reach Santa. If only we could do something big—like go on TV or something."

"How would we ever get on TV?" Cassie asked.

How? I knew exactly how!

"You guys!" I said. "My dad is the host of *Good Morning San Francisco*. Maybe he'll let me go on his show and tell Santa where we'll be this Christmas!"

"But the show is called *Good Morning San Francisco*, Michelle," Mandy said. "Not *Good Morning North Pole*."

"San Francisco is a big city!" I said. "Someone watching the show might know Santa and give him the message!"

I felt like doing a zillion cartwheels!

Just when I thought I was out of ideas I got a brand-new one. And this one was going to *work*!

Chapter Nine

"Dad?" I asked that night at dinner. "Can I be on *Good Morning San Francisco* tomorrow?"

"Don't you need a hit movie first, Michelle?" Joey joked. "Or a best-selling book?"

"Or a famous record?" Uncle Jesse teased.

"Why do you want to go on *Good Morning San Francisco*, Michelle?" Dad asked.

"Well, Dad," I started to explain, "you see—"

"Wait a minute," Dad interrupted. He

looked around the table. "Why don't I have the whole family on tomorrow? As part of our Christmas show!"

"Really?" D.J. squealed.

"Cool!" Stephanie cried.

Soon everyone was talking.

"I'll practice some Christmas songs to sing," Uncle Jesse announced.

"Not until we give the twins a bath!" Aunt Becky said.

Uncle Jesse, Aunt Becky, and the twins hurried out of the dining room. So did D.J. and Stephanie. They wanted to find something great to wear on the show tomorrow.

"I'll come up with some holiday jokes," Uncle Joey said, standing up.

Dad ruffled my hair. "Thanks, Michelle. Great idea."

My mouth was still open as Dad and Uncle Joey left the dining room. I was alone at the dinner table!

"Oh, well," I said, crushing a cracker into my soup. "I guess that means *yes!*"

"We're ready for our close-ups!" Uncle Joey said.

I giggled as he tugged the pom-pom on my Santa hat.

It was early Tuesday morning—two hours before school began. But I was too excited to be sleepy. That's because the whole Tanner family was standing in a real-live television studio. We were all wearing Santa hats, too. That was my idea!

As we waited to go on camera, I looked around. People wearing headsets and carrying clipboards were running around the busy studio. There were tons of lights hanging from the ceiling and wires all over the floor.

Three TV cameras were pointed at my

dad. He was standing behind a counter making a gingerbread house.

"How cool is this?" Stephanie whispered to me.

"Way cool!" I whispered back.

But even cooler was what I was planning to do—get my message to Santa Claus!

Carolyn Dawson, the producer of *Good Morning San Francisco,* walked over. "Nice hats, you guys," she said in a quiet voice. "Now, here's what you'll be doing on the show. . . ."

Everyone inched closer to Carolyn.

"Danny will finish the cooking segment and introduce you all," she told us. "Then I'll give you a signal to walk onto the set."

The pom-poms on our hats bounced up and down as we nodded.

"First Joey will say something funny,"

Carolyn went on. "Then Jesse will play a Christmas song on his guitar."

Uncle Jesse lifted his guitar and smiled.

"Then, as the show closes," Carolyn said, "you'll all wave and say 'Merry Christmas' to the audience."

"Merry Christmas!" Alex yelled.

"Shh," Aunt Becky whispered. "Not yet, sweetie."

"Any questions?" Carolyn asked us.

I raised my hand. "Does Santa get this show in the North Pole?"

Carolyn smiled. "Well, you never know who might be watching *Good Morning San Francisco!*" She gave us a thumbs-up sign and walked away.

"How does my makeup look?" D.J. asked.

"Is my hair okay?" Stephanie said.

I watched my dad on the set. He was pressing gumdrops onto the creamy roof of the gingerbread house. He wiped his hands on his apron and smiled to the camera. "And that's all it takes to make a gingerbread house," he said to the camera. "But I'm going to need a lot of help eating it, so let's bring out some hungry Tanners!"

"You're on!" Carolyn called softly.

Dad called our names as we hurried over.

"Hey, Danny! What do elves learn when they go to school?" Uncle Joey asked.

"I don't know, Joey," Dad said. "What do elves learn?"

"The *elf*-abet!" Uncle Joey cried.

Dad groaned, but I thought it was funny!

Next Uncle Jesse picked up his guitar and sang "Have Yourself a Merry Little Christmas." When he finished Dad turned toward one of the middle cameras. "And now my family and I would like to wish each and every one of you a . . ."

"MERRY CHRISTMAS!" we all shouted and waved.

Then I stepped up to the middle camera. "If anyone out there knows where Santa Claus is, tell him the Tanners will be in Connecticut for Christmas! Greenwich, Connecticut!"

"Michelle!" Dad called.

"We're not the only ones!" I kept going. "My friend Louie Rizzoli is going to visit his grandpa. He lives in—"

"Michelle?" Dad interrupted. I felt his hand on my shoulder. "The show is over."

The bright lights flashed off. The crew started taking off their headsets. A voice over a loudspeaker said, "That's a wrap, everybody!"

"But, Dad!" I cried. "I didn't get to tell Santa where we'll be on Christmas!"

Follow the arrow and circle every other letter around the wreath. Then write the letters in the spaces below to get a message from Michelle! We did the first one to get you started.

H _ _ _ _ _
_ _ _ _ _ _ _ _ !

Created and produced by Parachute Publishing, L.L.C., published by HarperEntertainment. TM & © Warner Bros. Entertainment Inc. (s03). All rights reserved.

Dear Michelle
c/o HarperEntertainment
10 East 53rd Street
New York, NY 10022

FIRST
CLASS
POSTAGE
REQUIRED

Chapter Ten

"I can't believe it," I said after school that day. "I was on television today and I totally blew it!"

I walked out of the school building with Cassie, Mandy, and Louie. It was the last day before winter break. We were all carrying goodie bags that Mrs. Ramirez had given us. They were filled with chocolates and candy canes.

"It's not your fault, Michelle," Louie said. "There wasn't enough time to tell Santa where we'll be."

"We're both leaving San Francisco

tomorrow, Louie." I sighed. "And I don't know what else to do."

The four of us walked quietly until we reached a busy street. It was packed with people rushing in and out of stores, doing Christmas shopping.

"Ho, ho, ho!" a voice boomed. "Merrrry Christmas!"

I turned my head. A man in a red and white suit was ringing a bell in front of Mack's Hardware Store.

"Santa?" I wondered out loud.

But then I saw another guy in a red and white suit in front of Phipp's Department Store. And another in front of the Hobby Shop. And one more handing out menus in front of the taco place!

"Those are some of Santa's helpers," Mandy pointed out. "He's got a lot of them this time of year."

A helper waved at us as we walked by.

That's when it hit me like a ton of jingle bells. . . .

"You guys, why don't we ask the helpers to give our message to Santa?" I asked. "If Santa's the boss, they'll know how to reach him!"

Louie and I wrote our grandparents' names and addresses on a piece of notebook paper. When we were finished, we checked out the sidewalk Santas.

"Which one do we give it to?" Mandy asked.

"I want the best," I declared. "The best Santa's helper of them all!"

"How do we know which is best?" Louie asked.

I studied the Santa's helpers. They looked alike. Their ho-ho-hos even sounded alike.

"Hmmm. Maybe we can give them a little test," I said. "We can ask them a bunch of cool questions about Santa Claus. The one who knows the most about him wins!"

"Cool!" Louie said, grinning. "And the prize is giving our message to the *real* Santa Claus!"

We thought of a few questions to ask Santa's helpers. Then we ran over to the hardware Santa.

"Quick. Santa has a wife," I said. "Tell us her name!"

The hardware Santa looked surprised. "Errr," he said, scratching his head, "is it . . . Mrs. Claus?"

"That's it!" I shouted.

"Reindeer," Louie whispered to me. "Ask him about the reindeer!"

I looked at the hardware Santa. "Name all of Santa's reindeer," I said.

"No problem," he said. "Comet . . . Cupid . . . Prancer . . . and the one with the red nose . . . what's his name?"

I looked sideways at my friends. How

could a Santa's helper not know the most famous reindeer of all?

"It's Rudolph," Cassie told him. "But nice try."

We moved on to the taco Santa next.

But when we asked him how many times Santa checked his list, he didn't have a clue!

"You got me," he said with a laugh. "Six? Seven?"

"Twice," Mandy said.

And when we asked him how many reindeer Santa had, he shrugged. "Six? Seven?" he asked.

"Thanks anyway," I said with a smile.

The hobby shop Santa's helper flunked, too. So did the helper giving out gingerbread smoothie samples. They couldn't name Santa's reindeer either.

There was only one Santa left—the one in front of Phipp's Department Store.

"Ho, ho, ho!" he shouted as we walked over.

"Would you mind taking a Santa test?" I asked him.

"There's nothing more I'd rather do!" he said with a jolly grin.

"Then here's the first question," I said. "Who helps Santa in his workshop?"

Santa's helper tugged at his beard as he thought. "That would be his elves," he said. Then he leaned over and whispered, "In fact, if you listen real close, you'll hear the bells on their shoes as they run around the workshop!"

"Really?" I asked.

"Neat!" Cassie gasped.

Santa's helper answered three more questions perfectly. But then came the trickiest question of all. . . .

"Can you name all of Santa's reindeer?" I asked.

Santa's helper took a deep breath. "Hmmm, that's a tough one. . . ."

I held my breath. The Phipp's Santa was our last chance to get a message to Santa. Would he pass the test?

Chapter Eleven

Santa's helper smiled. His eyes twinkled as he recited each and every reindeer's name! "Dasher, Dancer, Prancer, Vixen, Comet, Cupid, Donner, Blitzen . . . and Rudolph, of course!" he said. "How's that?"

"Wow!" I shouted. "You've got the job!"

"Ho, ho, ho!" Santa's helper replied. "What job?"

"To deliver our message to the real Santa!" Louie said.

"Okay. What is your message to Santa?" the helper asked.

"My grandma's address in Connecticut,"

I explained. "And Louie's grandfather's address in Denver."

"We want to make sure Santa finds us on Christmas Eve," Louie went on. "Since we'll be away and all."

Santa's helper studied the paper. Then he looked up at us and said, "Santa finds *all* good kids on Christmas Eve. No matter where they are."

"I've heard that one before," Louie mumbled.

"But how do we know for sure?" I asked the helper.

"How?" Santa's helper asked. Then he gave us a wink. "Why, you just have to believe!"

"Wow!" I gasped. "That's exactly what my dad told me."

"Then your dad is a very wise man!" the helper said. "But I'll give Santa the message, just to be sure."

"Thanks, sir!" Louie said. But his eyes were already on something else. "Check out the awesome bike in the store window!"

Louie, Mandy, and Cassie ran to check out the bike. But I didn't. I had something else I wanted to talk to this Santa about—Grandma's sweater. Maybe he could help.

I told him the whole story.

"My grandma is going to hate it!" I finished. "What do I do now?"

Santa's helper looked into my eyes. "Your grandma is going to love the sweater, Michelle," he said. "Believe me, I know."

"How do you know?" I asked.

"Because it came from you." He leaned over and whispered, "And because Santa told me that blue is your grandma's favorite color!"

"He did?" I whispered back.

"Trust me," Santa's helper said. "And

have a merrrrrry Christmas. Ho, ho, ho!"

I smiled at Santa's helper. And as I ran to join my friends, I knew we had picked the *best*!

"Michelle!" Dad called. "The taxi is here. You'd better hurry!"

"Coming, Dad!" I called back.

It was Wednesday, Christmas Eve. But I wasn't going anywhere until I had left a little something for Santa. . . .

"Plate of cookies. Check," I said. "Map to Grandma's house. Check."

I made sure the cookies and the note were right by the fireplace. I had a feeling Santa wouldn't stop at an empty house. But it couldn't hurt to be prepared!

I also made sure Louie's telephone number in Denver was in my pocket. We'd promised to call each other if we had any Santa news.

"Michelle!" Dad called again. "Let's go!"

"Okay, Dad!" I buttoned my jacket and ran outside. Everyone was loading suitcases and duffel bags into two taxis. "Yippee!" I cheered. "We're going to Grandma's!"

I couldn't wait to see Grandma and give her the present I'd made. Now that I knew blue was her favorite color, I was sure she was going to love it!

All during the plane trip I couldn't stop smiling. Stephanie let me sit by the window for the whole trip. I even got a pair of silver wings to pin on my jacket. But when we got to Connecticut, my jacket wasn't warm enough. I had to bundle up in a bulky parka, hat, and gloves!

"I think I see Grandma looking out the window!" I told Stephanie as we walked up the path to Grandma's house.

I was holding my present for Grandma. Stephanie was holding hers. But then I noticed something weird about Stephanie's present. The wrapping paper was pink!

"How come you didn't wrap Grandma's present in Christmas paper?" I asked her.

"Because Grandma's favorite color is pink," Stephanie said with a shrug.

"Pink?" I stopped walking. "But Grandma's favorite color is blue . . . isn't it?"

I got my answer when Grandma swung open the door. The walls in the foyer were pink, so was the rug, and even the curtains at the end of the hall.

Oh, no! I thought. I can't do anything about Grandma's present now!

"There you are at last!" Grandma cried. "Welcome to an old-fashioned Christmas!"

I ran to Grandma and gave her a hug. She smelled like chocolate-chip cookies. And her short hair looked really nice!

After everyone got to hug Grandma, we walked into the house. It felt all warm and toasty inside. But when I saw the living room, I couldn't believe my eyes.

Grandma's tree was decorated with strings of popcorn, silver bells, handmade ornaments, and tons of candy canes. A fire was crackling in the fireplace, and there were stockings for all of us hanging on the banister.

"It's exactly as I remember it," Dad sighed. "An old-fashioned Christmas tree for an old-fashioned Christmas."

"That's the idea, Danny," Grandma said. "Now, why don't you all take your bags upstairs so we can start celebrating Christmas Eve?"

We all lugged our bags up the staircase. D.J., Stephanie, and I shared Dad's old room. The walls were covered with posters for rock groups with funny names—like Three Dog Night and K.C. and the Sunshine Band.

Just as my tummy started to rumble, Grandma called us down to dinner. And I mean *dinner*!

We ate goose, buttered peas and carrots, roasted potatoes, and acorn squash. And for dessert we had hot apple pie with vanilla ice cream!

"I'm so stuffed, I can't move!" Uncle Joey groaned.

"Well, you'd better get over it quickly, Joe." Grandma rubbed her hands together. "Because we're going caroling!"

In a flash we were bundled up again and standing outside. Uncle Jesse started strumming his guitar.

"What song do we sing first?" he asked.

"'Santa Claus Is Coming to Town!'" I cried.

"Is that your favorite, Michelle?" Grandma asked.

I looked up at the night sky for any sign

of Santa's sleigh. "It is now, Grandma!" I said.

But as we began to sing at the top of our lungs, something totally awesome happened. It began to snow!

Even if I don't get the scooter, I thought, it's still going to be a great Christmas!

I opened my mouth and caught a snowflake on my tongue.

It doesn't get any better than this!

Chapter Twelve

"Michelle, wake up! Wake up!"

My eyes popped open. Nicky and Alex were standing by my bed. They were hopping up and down like kangaroos.

"It's Christmas Day!" Alex said.

"Look out the window, Michelle!" Nicky cried.

I climbed out of bed and ran to the window. I pulled up the shade and gasped. The streets and cars and rooftops were completely covered with snow!

"It's a white Christmas!" I cheered.

Nicky grabbed my hand. "Time for

presents!" he said, tugging me toward the stairs.

Our slippers thumped on the steps as we ran downstairs. Everyone was already in the living room and standing in front of the Christmas tree.

"Merry Christmas, sleepyhead!" Dad called to me.

Then they each took one giant step to the side and shouted, "Merry Christmas, Michelle!"

I blinked my eyes once, twice, even three times. Standing right under the tree was a shiny silver scooter with pink wheels!

"It's true, it's true!" I shouted as I jumped up and down. "All you have to do is believe. Santa found me!"

"Santa *does* come to Connecticut, Michelle," Grandma chuckled.

"I know," I cried as I ran to the scooter. "And he brought me just what I wanted!"

"There's something else for you, Michelle," Dad said. "But this present isn't from Santa. It's from me."

Dad pointed to a wooden *Nutcracker* soldier under the tree. There was a white envelope stuck between his teeth.

"Open it, Michelle," Aunt Becky said.

"What is it?" I asked, taking the envelope. Then I reached inside and pulled out—

"Tickets to *The Nutcracker* ballet!" I cried.

"In New York City!" Dad added. "It's less than an hour away!"

"Stephanie and I are going, too," D.J. said.

"Yeah!" Stephanie said. "No way would we miss a trip to New York!"

"Thanks, Dad!" I wrapped my arms around his waist and squeezed. "I always wanted to see *The Nutcracker* on a real live stage!"

"Me tutu!" Uncle Joey joked.

"So, Michelle," Uncle Jesse said. "I guess Santa came through for you after all."

"You bet he did," I said. "Just like always." Then I remembered Louie and our promise! "Dad? Can I call Louie in Denver? Please?"

"Denver?" Dad asked. "That's another long-distance call."

"I know," I said. "But Denver, Colorado, is a lot closer than the North Pole!"

"Oh, go ahead and call Louie!" Grandma said with a grin. "It's Christmas!"

"Thanks, Grandma!" I said.

I ran upstairs for Louie's number. Then I ran to the phone in Grandma's bedroom and dialed.

"Merry Christmas," a gruff voice answered. "Who's this?"

I figured it was Louie's grandpa!

"Merry Christmas, Mr. Rizzoli!" I said. "This is Michelle Tanner in Connecticut. I'd like to speak to Louie."

"What time is it over there?" Mr. Rizzoli asked.

I glanced at the clock radio on Grandma's night table. "About eight-thirty," I answered.

"Well, it's six-thirty in the morning over here!" Mr. Rizzoli said.

"Oops," I said. "Sorry!"

"That's okay," Mr. Rizzoli said. "Louie's been up since *five*-thirty!"

Mr. Rizzoli called Louie.

"Hi, Michelle," Louie said over the phone.

"Louie, guess what?" I asked. "Santa gave me the silver scooter with the pink wheels. And Dad got me tickets to *The Nutcracker* in New York City!"

"Santa gave me the remote-controlled

car I wanted!" Louie exclaimed. "And it's snowing!"

"Here, too!" I cried.

"Wow, Michelle," Louie said. "This Christmas rocks!"

I heard D.J. calling my name downstairs. "Uh-oh," I told Louie. "I think it's time to give Grandma her sweater. Her itchy blue sweater."

"Good luck," Louie said. "And Merry Christmas!"

I hung up and ran downstairs. Grandma had just opened Aunt Becky's sachets.

"They smell heavenly!" Grandma said. "Thank you, Becky. Thank you, Jesse."

I watched as Grandma opened her other gifts. She loved D.J.'s scarf. And Stephanie's bird feeder. And the twins' Christmas drawings. Even the earrings Uncle Joey had made out of red and white candy canes.

"Michelle," Dad whispered. "Your turn."

"Okay, Dad." I picked up my wrapped present and gave it to Grandma.

"Hmm. What could it be?" Grandma asked. She ripped off the Christmas wrapping paper.

"It's okay if you don't like it," I said as she opened the box. "I didn't know that pink—"

"Oh, I *love* it!" Grandma pulled out the sweater.

"You . . . do?" I squeaked. "Even if it's a little . . . itchy?"

Grandma waved her hand. "Oh, I'll just wash it in Woolite. It won't be itchy," she said. "I love it because it's from you!"

"Really?" I asked.

"Really, truly!" Grandma said. "And besides, blue is my favorite color! How did you know?"

I glanced at Stephanie.

She shrugged. "I guess I was wrong."

"Thank you, Michelle!" Grandma said. Then she reached out and gave me a big Christmas hug!

It's true! I thought as I squeezed my grandma. Not only does Santa know where all good kids are on Christmas . . . he knows *everything*!

"Merry Christmas, Santa," I whispered. "Wherever you are!"

Hi, I'm Michelle Tanner!

I write the advice column for my school newspaper, the Third-Grade Buzz. I love writing letters—and getting them! Did you ever wonder how the mail gets delivered? Find out how it's done on the next page. And while you're at it, check out the fun facts I learned about mail, too!

(1) First, you write your letter, address the envelope, and put a stamp on it. The stamp is how you pay for the delivery!

Did you know if a stamp has a mistake on it, it could be worth a lot of money? A stamp collector once paid 3.8 million dollars for one stamp!

(2) Then you put your letter in the mailbox, and the mail carrier collects it from the box and brings it to the local post office.

Did you know mail used to be delivered by horse? Mailmen would ride all over the country just so people could get their letters. It was called the Pony Express.

(3) At the post office, postal workers sort the mail by the address you put on your envelope. Then the mail is sent to the post office closest to the address on your envelope.

Did you know that the post office sorts more than 200 billion pieces of mail each year? That's a lot of letters!

4) Finally, the mail is given to another mail carrier, who brings your letter right to your friend's house.

Did you know the average mail carrier delivers more than 2,300 letters a day? Wow! That takes a lot of muscle!

So you see why it's really important to know what goes on an envelope? It's the only way the mailman can know where your letter is going!

(1) Write your return address (that's where you live) in the upper left corner.

(2) In the middle of the envelope, write the name and the address of the person your letter is going to.

(3) Then stick on a first-class stamp in the upper right corner and you're all set!

See the example below:

(1) Mandy Metz
1230 Sunshine Lane
San Francisco, CA 55555

(3) stamp
goes
here

(2) Michelle Tanner
c/o HarperEntertainment
10 East 53rd Street
New York, NY 10022

Do you need some advice—or want to ask me a question? I may able to answer you in one of my future columns! I wish I could answer all of your letters, but I get too many! I would still love to hear from you. Write to me, Michelle, at:

Dear Michelle
c/o HarperEntertainment
10 East 53rd Street
New York, NY 10022

You can use the cool postcard in this book. It already has the address on it!

Here's a sneak peek at

#3 Who Will Be My Valentine?

"This is so exciting!" Cassie said at lunch. "A boy likes a girl in our class. Who do you think Mr. Shy Guy is, Michelle?"

I shrugged. "I don't know. I just want to help him out and answer his question."

"Let me see the letter again," Mandy said.

I pulled the latest "Dear Michelle" letter from my backpack and handed it to her.

Mandy looked at the letter. "Hmm. The girl Shy Guy thinks is nice is smart and good at sports. She has strawberry-blond hair and blue eyes. And she has a big friendly family."

"I still have no idea who it could be," I said.

"Wait a minute!" Cassie shouted. She stared at me.

"What?" I asked. "Did you figure it out?"

Cassie shook her head. "I don't know who Shy Guy is," she said, "but I do know who he thinks is nice." She pointed at me. "You!"

"No way," I said. "It could be anyone in our class." I could feel my face turning red.

"Maybe Cassie is right, Michelle," Mandy said. "You have strawberry-blond hair. You're smart and good at sports. You have a big family. . . ."

I was glad when the bell rang. Mrs. Ramirez brought us back to class, and we started working on our Valentine's Day cards.

I walked up to the supply table to get some glue. When I returned to my desk, there was a piece of folded white paper on my seat.

24
TED   30⊊ 784

It was a note! I opened it up and read it.

Dear Michelle,
Roses are red
Violets are blue
Monkeys are cute
And so are you!
    —Your Secret Admirer

I stared at the last three words. Wow! I thought. Mandy and Cassie are right! I do have a secret admirer.
    I glanced around the room.
    But who is it?